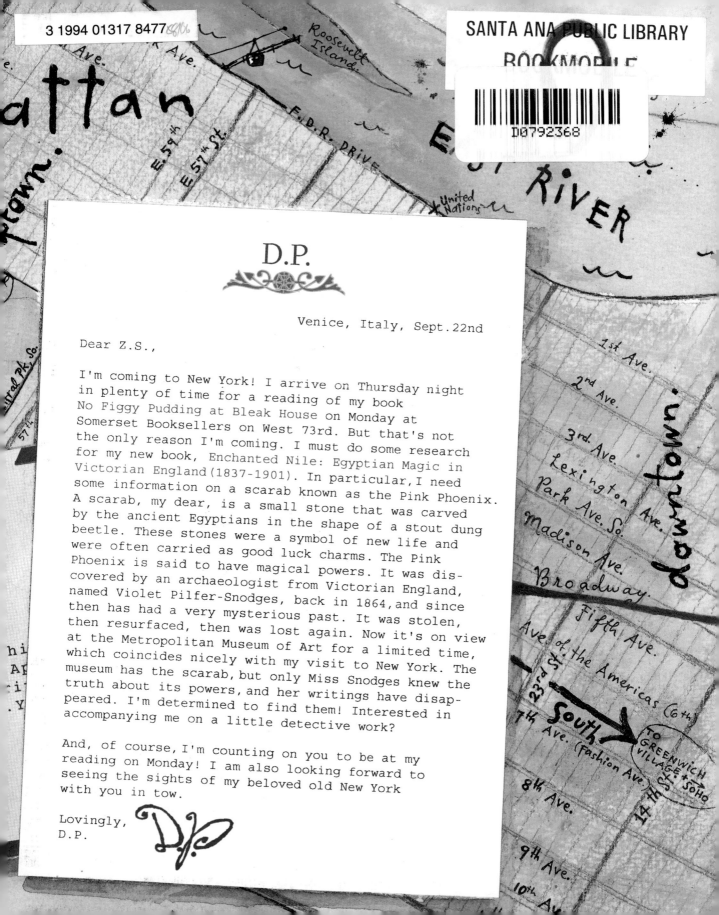

D.P.

Venice, Italy, Sept.22nd

Dear Z.S.,

I'm coming to New York! I arrive on Thursday night in plenty of time for a reading of my book No Figgy Pudding at Bleak House on Monday at Somerset Booksellers on West 73rd. But that's not the only reason I'm coming. I must do some research for my new book, Enchanted Nile: Egyptian Magic in Victorian England (1837-1901). In particular, I need some information on a scarab known as the Pink Phoenix. A scarab, my dear, is a small stone that was carved by the ancient Egyptians in the shape of a stout dung beetle. These stones were a symbol of new life and were often carried as good luck charms. The Pink Phoenix is said to have magical powers. It was discovered by an archaeologist from Victorian England, named Violet Pilfer-Snodges, back in 1864, and since then has had a very mysterious past. It was stolen, then resurfaced, then was lost again. Now it's on view at the Metropolitan Museum of Art for a limited time, which coincides nicely with my visit to New York. The museum has the scarab, but only Miss Snodges knew the truth about its powers, and her writings have disappeared. I'm determined to find them! Interested in accompanying me on a little detective work?

And, of course, I'm counting on you to be at my reading on Monday! I am also looking forward to seeing the sights of my beloved old New York with you in tow.

Lovingly,
D.P.

This book is lovingly dedicated to the memory of:

My dear father, George L. Mauner,
who showed me the magic —Claudia Mauner

and

My treasured sister, Vera Olvey Costello —Elisa Smalley

Our thanks to Rosemary Stimola, Lisa McGuinness, Victoria Rock,
Mary Beth Fiorentino, Marianne Mauner, and Robert Smalley.

Text © 2006 by Claudia Mauner and Elisa Smalley.
Illustrations © 2006 by Claudia Mauner.
All rights reserved.

Book design by Mary Beth Fiorentino.
Typeset in Filosofia.
The illustrations in this book were rendered in
watercolor and India ink.
Manufactured in Hong Kong.

Library of Congress Cataloging-in-Publication Data
Mauner, Claudia.
Zoe Sophia in New York : the mystery of the Pink Phoenix papers / by Claudia Mauner
and Elisa Smalley; illustrated by Claudia Mauner.
p. cm.
Summary: Zoe and her great-aunt do research in New York to solve a mystery
surrounding a pink scarab at the Metropolitan Museum of Art.
ISBN-13: 978-0-8118-4877-0
ISBN-10: 0-8118-4877-9
[1. Scarabs—Fiction. 2. Great-aunts—Fiction. 3. New York (N.Y.)—Fiction.
4. Mystery and detective stories.] I. Smalley, Elisa. II. Title
PZ7.M44513Zm 2006
[Fic]—dc22
2004026190

Distributed in Canada by Raincoast Books
9050 Shaughnessy Street, Vancouver, British Columbia V6P 6E5

10 9 8 7 6 5 4 3 2 1

Chronicle Books LLC
85 Second Street, San Francisco, California 94105

www.chroniclekids.com

Zoe Sophia in New York

The Mystery of the Pink Phoenix Papers

By Claudia Mauner and Elisa Smalley · Illustrated by Claudia Mauner

chronicle books · san francisco

My Room at the Antwerp:

My name is Zoe Sophia and I am nine years old. I'm an explorer at heart, but my home is New York City, on the Upper West Side. I live in a building called the Antwerp. Our apartment is 8B. My favorite color is purple and my favorite person in the whole world is my great aunt Dorothy Pomander, whom I visited last year in Venice. D. P. is a famous writer, which I hope to be myself one day.

Dorothy sends me e-mail, but when she has something important to say, she sends me snail mail from Venice. I just got a letter today, announcing her arrival tomorrow!!! I can't wait. Visits with Dorothy are always full of surprises.

Mickey is a homebody here in New York. He loves to watch me feed my guppy, Gordon.

My Class at the Wildendorf School

My school bus is the 86th Street crosstown bus, which I catch at the southeast corner of 86th and West End. (In New York City, lots of kids take city buses to school.) At Broadway and 86th we pick up my best friend, Alexa. I always save her a seat. At Central Park West, Angela Vanderhuff gets on the bus. She always rides the bus standing in fifth position.

Our school is the Wildendorf School for the Exceptionally Curious, a school for thirsty little minds. It is directly across from the Metropolitan Museum of Art on Fifth Avenue. Our teacher, Ms. Fionnula Feinschmecker, has the millefiori paperweight I brought her from Venice on her desk.

Thursday Afternoon: Ballet Class

Alexa and I have ballet after school today. Angela is in the class too. The ballet mistress is Madame Ludmila, who came here a gazillion years ago from the Bolshoi Ballet in Moscow. She wears a ton of black eyeliner and pounds a stick on the floor to keep time. *"I raz, i dva, i tri* (and 1 and 2 and 3)." She counts in Russian.

Today I can barely focus on my port de bras. All I can think about is Dorothy's arrival tonight! She'll be here for a whole week! I even got us a pair of tickets for the New York City Ballet's performance of Stravinsky's *Firebird* at Lincoln Center for Saturday night. Blossom, our Jamaican housekeeper, is picking me up after ballet. We are going shopping for some very special ingredients for Dorothy's welcome dinner!

Welcome

Later that Night: Welcome Dinner

Dorothy is famished when she finally arrives. Luckily, Blossom has prepared gobs of jerk chicken, complete with mango chutney and all the trimmings—a recipe straight out of her new cookbook on Jamaican cuisine called *Come Nam Yuh Bickle*, which means "soup's on."

My parents barely have time to kiss Dorothy hello before rushing off in a cloud of perfume and aftershave. (My mother is the travel editor at *Savoir Faire* magazine, and they're always having these galas.) "How delightful to be back in my city of so many years!" exclaims Dorothy with gusto as we sit down to enjoy our feast and toast her arrival.

Dorothy!!!

Just then, we hear the buzzer. It's Tibor from 7B—he is always borrowing a clove of garlic or something. He ends up staying for dinner, telling tales of his days as a tightrope walker in the National Hungarian Circus.

The Card Reading

Tibor has gypsy blood and is a big believer in *mulatschag*, which is Hungarian for "living it up." After dinner, he offers to give Dorothy a Tarot card reading. She is delighted. We dim the lights and he takes out a worn pack of cards, fanning them out on a silk cloth. He asks Dorothy to select a card. She pulls one out and turns it over to reveal a bird surrounded by fire. "Aha!" Tibor exclaims, "The phoenix!"

Dorothy and I are both thinking the same thing:
the *Pink Phoenix*. Tibor explains that a phoenix is a mythical
bird that perishes in flames only to rise again from its ashes.
"You are on a quest," he says, "the lady must face south for answers!"

We get a little spooked by all this, so Blossom whips us up a batch of banana
fritters to calm our nerves.

It is very late by the time we finish, and Dorothy says she needs matchsticks to
keep her eyes open. Victor the doorman calls a cab to take her to her hotel in
Greenwich Village. Tomorrow after school we will go directly to the Metropolitan
Museum of Art to see the famous *Pink Phoenix*.

Friday: The Met

You need three days to see the whole Met, but we are only going to the Egyptian wing. We pass through halls of jewelry and slabs of stone engraved with Egyptian symbols called hieroglyphics. At last we find it: the *Pink Phoenix!* It is in a case by itself. Its rose color glows against black velvet. A gold plaque reads as follows:

THE PINK PHOENIX

LIMITED TIME ONLY

FRED & GINGER DANCING SHOES

THE NAME OF THIS SCARAB COMES FROM ITS UNIQUE COLOR AND THE ENGRAVING OF A PHOENIX ON ITS UNDERSIDE. THE PINK PHOENIX IS ONE OF THE GREAT TREASURES OF THE 18TH DYNASTY. DATING FROM CIRCA 1350 B.C., IT WAS ONE OF THE PRIZED POSSESSIONS OF QUEEN NEFERTITI, WHO BELIEVED IT TO HAVE MAGICAL POWERS. IT WAS DISCOVERED IN 1864 BY AN ENGLISH ARCHAEOLOGIST, VIOLET PILFER-SNODGES, WHOSE JOURNAL WAS LOST IN A LONDON HOUSEFIRE. STOLEN FROM LONDON'S VICTORIA & ALBERT MUSEUM IN 1922, THE SCARAB RESURFACED YEARS LATER AT AN AUCTION IN BANGLADESH.

"I'm certain that at least one copy of that diary survives,"
says Dorothy as we leave the museum. Ravenous, we buy two falafels
at a stand. "Fit for a pharaoh!" says Dorothy with glee. "I must find
that journal," she muses between mouthfuls, "but where?" It's late now
and we must hurry so I can still show Dorothy the Penguin House.

The Penguin House

The Penguin House in Central Park Zoo off Fifth Avenue is a great place to go when you need to think. It's dark and quiet in there. Dorothy and I watch the penguins dive and zoom under water. They stop to rub noses with us up against the glass. "Quite the opposite of the regal phoenix!" Dorothy chuckles. We could stay here forever, but Dorothy says we must get going, as we have a dinner reservation at her favorite restaurant off Lexington Avenue.

Outside the Penguin House, I step on something smooth in the gravel. It is a playing card—the jack of clubs. On the back of the card, there is an image of a winged bird, rising from the flames—a phoenix! Dorothy says that jacks, clubs, and phoenixes are all rife with meaning, so I slip the card in my backpack. "A trip to the library will help us interpret these signs," Dorothy says with a wink.

Dinner at Mme. Roulade's

What makes Mme. Roulade's so special is that Dorothy's dear friend Mr. Kirk Irving is the pianist there. As he plays "Moonlight on the Nile," I see Dorothy's eyes widen behind her thick glasses. "Look!" she gasps, pointing to a matchbook on the table. "A phoenix! Right on the flap."

There is no doubt, phoenixes all over are definitely a sign—
but of WHAT??? I tuck the matchbook in my backpack.
We decide to clear our heads and take in the latest Czech
film, *Cirkus Bláznů* ("Circus of Fools"), at the Paris theatre.
I feel very grown-up watching a movie with subtitles.

Saturday: N.Y. Public Library

First thing next morning, Dorothy and I head to the New York Public Library, armed with pencils and note cards.

We climb the steps to the entrance between Patience and Fortitude, the two great marble lions that lie sphinx-like in front of the library, guarding the secrets within. "Doing research, my dear, is much like going on an archaeological dig," Dorothy whispers as we enter the great hall. "Finding just the right tidbit is as thrilling as putting the last piece in a puzzle."

Here is what we discover:
① Ordinary playing cards come from the ancient Tarot cards.
② The Jack of Clubs = the Prince of wands in the Tarot deck.

③ All but ONE copy of the famous journal known as "The Pink Phoenix Papers" were destroyed in a fire in 1932. It has never been found...
④ Dachshunds were the Royal Canines of the Pharaohs.

"Dachshunds are far more than mere low-slung beasts, and this proves it," says Dorothy.

"Wands are a fire sign," she adds, "so we're on the right track. The phoenix, too, represents fire."

"Could this be connected with the fire that destroyed those papers?" I wonder out loud.

"Precisely," nods Dorothy. "But what of the prince of wands? Where does he come in???" Uggh! I wonder if archaeology is as frustrating as research!?

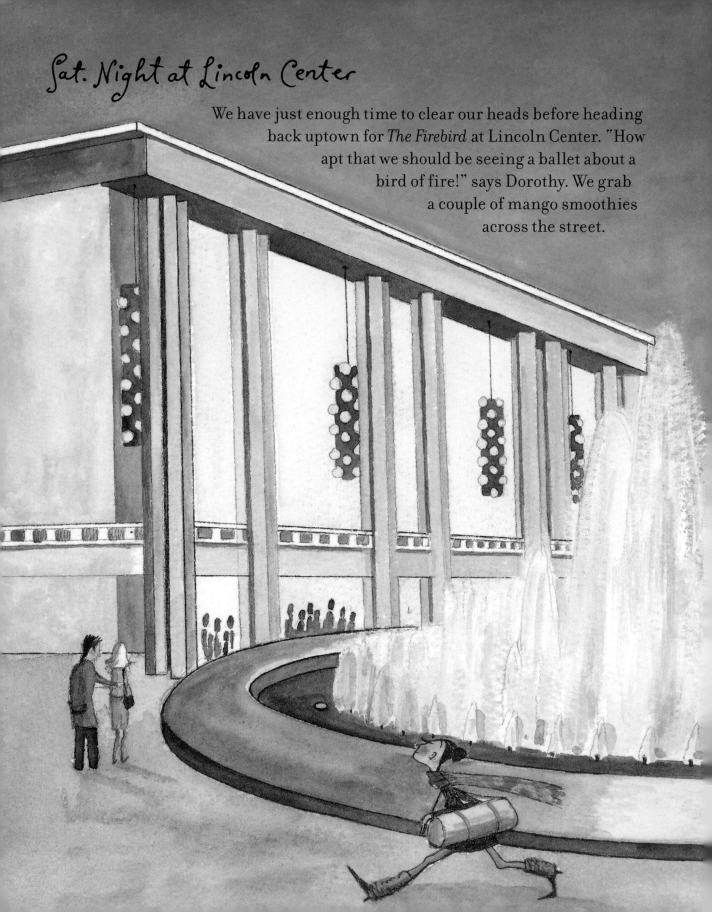

Sat. Night at Lincoln Center

We have just enough time to clear our heads before heading back uptown for *The Firebird* at Lincoln Center. "How apt that we should be seeing a ballet about a bird of fire!" says Dorothy. We grab a couple of mango smoothies across the street.

From the fountain, we have a perfect view of Chagall's paintings inside the
Metropolitan Opera House. It is getting dark and the fountain is lit up from inside.

The ballet is thrilling. Dorothy and I are riveted from Stravinsky's
first fiery note to the last curtain call. "A fitting finale
to a day of discovery," says Dorothy.

Greenwich Village (pronounced "Gren-itch")

Washington Square Park

Nothing ever closes downtown, so it's the perfect place to spend a Sunday looking for clues. The Village is on the southern end of Manhattan, and south is where we want to go. It's a funky part of the city. We walk from Dorothy's hotel through Washington Square Park on our way to the art supply store down on Canal Street.

Canal Street

Pearl Paint is five stories high. I need a new scrapbook, and Dorothy needs cartridges for her fountain pen. We stop to smell the erasers. "Heavenly!" Dorothy exclaims. The colored pencils have names like "aubergine" and "coffee bean." I buy one called "scarab green."

Chinatown

Canal Street stretches through Chinatown. It is loaded with teeny shops that sell everything from sunglasses to luggage. Dorothy and I buy a pair of matching Pino Raton handbags for four dollars—perfect for keeping our supplies in.

SOHO
(stands for "south of Houston—pronounced "Howston")

Somehow, we find ourselves on Prince Street. Dorothy stops short. "Look!" she says, pointing to a small, secondhand bookshop. "The symbol above the door is a phoenix!" Etched on the glass door it says Phoenix Secondhand Bookshop. "Prince Street," I say. "The playing card! The jack of clubs equals the prince of wands!" Dorothy squeezes my hand as we enter the shop.

Phoenix Bookshop

Entering the bookshop is like stepping into another world. We rummage for hours. I find a first edition *Harriet the Spy,* my favorite book of all time. Dorothy buys it for me. As I look over the shelves of kids' books, one book catches my eye. It's spine is frayed.

**THE EXOTIC TRAVEL DIARY OF:
VIOLET PILFER-SNODGES**

1863 – 1865

COMPLETE
AND UNABRIDGED

When I pry the book loose,
it just about falls apart in
my hands. I blow away the dust
to find a portrait of a lady wearing
a pith helmet. A brooch at her high-
collared throat glows pink—a scarab!
THE PINK PHOENIX!!!

"Criminey!" I practically fall over, handing
Dorothy the book. She reads the title: *The Exotic
Travel Diary of Violet Pilfer-Snodges 1863–1865*. Then she
whispers, "Zoe Sophia Sherlock—you've done it! You've
found the missing volume that will reveal the *Pink
Phoenix's* magic powers! Congratulations, my dear, and many
thanks. You have the magic touch the true scholar needs!"

Monday: Empire State Building

Dorothy's reading at Somerset Booksellers was a smash. Everyone came. Even Mickey was allowed in. After the big event, Dorothy and I had something very important to do.

The Empire State Building (Fifth Avenue and 34th Street), was once the tallest building in the world. The elevators shoot up like rockets, making us queasy. It is very windy up there. "Nothing like a bird's-eye view to give you some perspective," Dorothy says.

The city lights sparkle like tiny gems. We huddle together to keep warm. Looking past Greenwich Village, Dorothy says, "Now I understand why Tibor said to look south for answers. South is also where the Twin Towers once stood. I am quite certain, my dear, that like the phoenix, something magnificent will rise there from the ashes."

"Tomorrow I'll be seeing this from my airplane window and thinking of you," Dorothy says. I hug her tight. "Don't worry," she adds, "you and I have the whole world to explore."